FREDDIE
THE FLYER

To my family, to my coauthor, Danielle, for her years of patience and coaching, to Audrea for her beautiful artwork, to my aviation mentors and to all those who have supported me throughout my years of flying — FC

To Fred and Miki for being my Inuvik family. And thank you to the NWT Arts Council for making it possible for us to create together. — DMC

To the memory of Gwich'in and Inuvialuit pioneers, Thank You — ALW

Text copyright © 2023 by Fred Carmichael and Danielle Metcalfe-Chenail
Illustrations copyright © 2023 by Audrea Loreen-Wulf

Tundra Books, an imprint of Tundra Book Group, a division of Penguin Random House of Canada Limited

Library and Archives Canada Cataloguing in Publication

Title: Freddie the flyer / Danielle Metcalfe-Chenail and Fred Carmichael ; Audrea Loreen-Wulf, illustrator.
Names: Metcalfe-Chenail, Danielle, author. | Carmichael, Fred, author. | Loreen-Wulf, Audrea, illustrator.
Identifiers: Canadiana (print) 20220453306 | Canadiana (ebook) 20220453357 |
ISBN 9781774880807 (hardcover) | ISBN 9781774880814 (EPUB)
Subjects: LCSH: Carmichael, Fred—Juvenile literature. | LCSH: Air pilots—Canada—Biography—Juvenile
literature. | CSH: First Nations air pilots—Canada—Biography—Juvenile literature. | LCGFT:
Biographies. | LCGFT: Autobiographies. | LCGFT: Picture books.
Classification: LCC TL540.C44 M48 2023 | DDC j629.13092—dc23

Published simultaneously in the United States of America by Tundra Books of Northern New York, an imprint of Tundra Book Group, a division of Penguin Random House of Canada Limited

Library of Congress Control Number: 2022948554

Edited by Samantha Swenson
Designed by Sophie Paas-Lang
The artwork in this book was created with acrylic paint on canvas to capture the light and colors of Canada's Western Arctic.
Blank frames: Adobe Stock/prosotphoto; Adobe Stock/rangizzz.
The text was set in Sofia Pro and Adobe Caslon Pro.

Printed in China

www.penguinrandomhouse.ca

1 2 3 4 5   27 26 25 24 23

Penguin
Random House
TUNDRA BOOKS

FREDDIE
THE FLYER

WRITTEN BY
FRED CARMICHAEL AND
DANIELLE METCALFE-CHENAIL

ILLUSTRATED BY
AUDREA LOREEN-WULF

tundra

JANUARY
Videetoh Goojìidhàt
Hiqiññatchiaq

When Freddie was little, he hunted caribou with his family in the mountains. One day, he spotted a plane overhead. His heart soared. That night, as he slept on spruce boughs under the northern lights, he dreamed of flying. But that dream felt bigger than the whole Arctic.

FEBRUARY

Nohjuu ts'an
Uvluqtuhiinarvik

Freddie went to school in the tiny town of
Aklavik. He was half Scottish-Irish, half Gwich'in
and one hundred percent shy. But watching
fighter pilots save the day in Hollywood movies,
he imagined he was a hero, slicing the sky in a
Spitfire. But that was impossible . . . right?

MARCH

Echee zrìi'
Kivgalungniarvik

At ten, Freddie left school to help his family on the trapline, but his heart was in the sky. When a plane delivered supplies to their bush camp, he touched his dream for the first time. But how to become a pilot? At sixteen, he had the answer: earn money and go to flying school. So Freddie washed dishes, dug ditches and helped build a top secret radar base. His parents worried, though: Freddie's dream was bigger than anything they could imagine.

APRIL

Tadhaa zrii

Aukharvia

Freddie found school hard in the big city, but he loved flying more than anything. And his teachers helped him. He became a wizard at reading the weather and fantastic at fixing things. He earned his pilot's license and flew home in his very own plane.

MAY
Gwilyuu zrìi'
Qaukkiqqivik

He used that plane to serve the people of the Mackenzie Delta. One of these times, he flew a nurse and a pregnant woman to the hospital. The baby was born early — just as Freddie landed! He cranked the heat and radioed for an ambulance, keeping everyone safe and warm. The new mom was so grateful, she named her baby Fred!

JUNE

Vananh Adaghoo
Hikuirvik

Freddie soon moved to Inuvik, a brand-new town in the Delta that was growing as fast as his company. He built a hangar and an airstrip and trained local people in lots of different aviation jobs, such as pilot, mechanic and flight attendant.

JULY

Vananh yidichuu

Qilalukkiarvik

One time, Freddie had an engine fail on his way back from Tuktoyaktuk. He glided down safely beside the Mackenzie River. He had rations, an axe, plenty of water and twenty-four hours of daylight. But no radio to call for help — and he was staring at great big grizzly tracks! After a day and a half, Freddie thought he'd have to build a raft and then bushwhack to safety. Luckily, his friend appeared in a floatplane. He said to Freddie, "You're flying us home, kid."

AUGUST

Vananh gwijidhitsik

Ahiarniarvik

Freddie would fly experts of all types around the Western Arctic. Together they studied the land and water; looked for traditional sites and trails; counted moose and muskox; and tracked beluga and bowhead whales. Freddie waved his wings at people in their bush camps below as they fished and gathered berries — always keeping an eye out in case someone needed help.

SEPTEMBER

Vananh ne'nidijaa

Ukiakr̂arvik

In the fall, Freddie would squeeze trappers and their dog teams into his plane. He'd take them out to their camps before freeze-up and collect them at Christmas with their fur hauls. There would be dogs howling and growling, and a whole lot of stink — even with all the vents open!

OCTOBER

Vàdzaih zrii'
Hikuvik

Winter comes early to the Arctic, and it can be both beautiful and brutal.

Freddie once rescued a prospector stranded on the Barren Lands. Other pilots tried to make it. Even Freddie was forced back by blizzards once, twice, three times. Finally, he braved the storm, dodged snow dunes and landed on a nearby frozen lake. Then he carried the prospector to the plane and flew him to the hospital just in time.

NOVEMBER

Divii zrii'
Anguniarvik

Freddie loved the Delta, so he started a flightseeing company to share it with visitors. They dipped their toes in the Arctic Ocean (in summer, of course!), raced on dogsleds and snow machines and puzzled over mysterious pingos. They looked for Arctic animals and topped off their adventures with a trip to the famous Igloo Church.

DECEMBER

Jideendoo ts'an
Qitchirvik

The shy Northern boy became a pilot, a father, a businessman and a leader. He worked with all the people of the Western Arctic — Gwich'in, Inuvialuit, Métis and others — and appreciated all those who helped him along the way.

Freddie's flying dreams grew up along with him and were now as big as the sky.

Freddie lives on the traditional territory of the Gwich'in and Inuvialuit peoples, so we felt it was important to include their terms. We worked with esteemed language keepers to navigate the questions of dialects, translations and spellings, but any errors that made it into the book rest with us.

Mahsi Cho to Anna Lee McLeod, Indigenous Language Instructor at Moose Kerr School in Aklavik and at the Gwich'in Renewable Resource Board, for the Gwich'in translations in this book.

Quyaininni to Inuvialuktun Language and Knowledge Keeper Lillian Elias and Language Teachers Susan Peffer and Dwayne Drescher for the translation of the months of the year in the Uummarmiutun dialect of Inuvialuktun.

JANUARY
Videetoh Goojìidhàt *Vi-day-toe Go-gee-that*
Hard month to get over
Hiqiññatchiaq *Hiqi-nit-chiaq*
The new sun

FEBRUARY
Nohjuu ts'an *No-jew T-sun*
Moving back [to] less [dark] days
Uvluqtuhiinarvik *Uv-luq-tu-hiin-ar-vik*
The time when the days get longer

MARCH
Echee zrìi' *Eh-chay Rrrr eee*
Eagle month
Kivgalungniarvik *Kiv-ga-lung-niar-vik*
The time to go muskratting

APRIL
Tadhaa zrii *Ta-the Rrrr eee*
Warm month
Aukharvia *Auk-har-via*
The thaw

MAY
Gwilyuu zrìi' *Gwill–lew Rrrr eee*
Snow crust month
Qaukkiqqivik *Qauk-kir-vik*
The time to go duck hunting

JUNE
Vananh Adaghoo *Va-nun Ada-hoe*
During that time, it [ducks] lay eggs
Hikuirvik *Hik-kuir-vik*
The time the ice breaks

JULY
Vananh yidichuu *Va-nun Yid-ee Chew*
During that time, birds lose feathers
Qilalukkiarvik *Qila-lu-gar-niar-vik*
The time to get beluga whales

AUGUST
Vananh gwijidhitsik *Va-nun Gw-ih Ji-thi-t-sick*
During that time, plants/trees turn red
Ahiarniarvik *Ahiar-niar-vik*
The time to get berries

SEPTEMBER
Vananh ne'nidijaa *Va-nun Nay-ni-di-jaaaa*
In that time, birds fly away
Ukiakr̃arvik *Ukiak-rar-vik*
Fall time

OCTOBER
Vàdzaih zrii' *Vad-z-eye Rrrr eee*
Caribou month
Hikuvik *Hik-u-vik*
The time when ice forms

NOVEMBER
Divii zrìi' *Di–vee Rrrr eee*
Sheep month
Anguniarvik *Angu-niar-vik*
The time to go hunting

DECEMBER
Jideendoo ts'an *Ji-day-n-doe T-sun*
Heading towards [the new year]
Qitchirvik *Qit-chir-vik*
The time to celebrate

FRED "FREDDIE" CARMICHAEL

Frederick James Carmichael was born in Aklavik, Northwest Territories (NWT), on May 6, 1935, and grew up on a remote trapline outside town. His mother, Caroline Kay, came from a long line of Gwich'in chiefs in the Mackenzie Delta region of the Western Arctic. His father, Frank Carmichael, was of Scottish-Irish descent and became a trapper and politician in the NWT.

Freddie went to Immaculate Conception Residential and Day School in Aklavik until he was ten years old. He left to help his family rebuild after their home burned down. Then when Freddie was sixteen, a pilot called Don Violette took him up for his first flight. It was Don who urged Freddie to go to flying school in Edmonton, Alberta, to pursue his aviation dreams.

Freddie worked hard to get his private and commercial pilot's licenses with the extra help of George Fletcher and Fred Way, his instructors at Gateway Aviation. Then he saved up for a Stinson Voyager of his very own.

Freddie returned to the North and set about making a career for himself in aviation. He began by serving the reindeer herders north of Aklavik doing aerial patrols, then cofounded Reindeer Air Service with Lyle Trimble.

Freddie expanded operations over the years, hiring and training other Indigenous pilots, mechanics, crew and staff in the area. He faced considerable challenges, both personal and professional, but Freddie loved flying too much — and felt too big a responsibility to his family and community — to quit for good. He went on to found other companies, including Antler Aviation, Western Arctic Air and Western Arctic Nature Tours.

Later, Freddie served as President of the Gwich'in Tribal Council and Chair of the Aboriginal Pipeline Group. For his inspiring accomplishments and service, Freddie is a Member of the Order of Canada, a recipient of the Métis NWT Order of the Sash and an inductee of Canada's Aviation Hall of Fame. He holds an Honorary Doctor of Laws from the University of Saskatchewan, and his hometown officially renamed the Aklavik Airport the Freddie Carmichael Airport.

Freddie is now eighty-eight years old and still flying a Cessna 170 on floats, wheels and skis from his home on Long Lake in Inuvik, NWT. He lives there with his wife, Miki O'Kane, and their dog, Shadow.